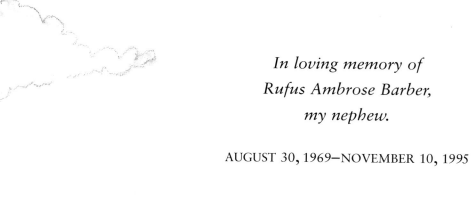

In loving memory of
Rufus Ambrose Barber,
my nephew.

AUGUST 30, 1969–NOVEMBER 10, 1995

PATRICIA POLACCO

I Can Hear the Sun

A MODERN MYTH

PUFFIN BOOKS

Lake Merritt, a lake right in the middle of Oakland, California, is magic for some, a place of rest for others, and home for many a wanderer. "Throwaway people," or so they're called, take up on its benches and call it home. Children play near the water while their tired mothers pull heavy air past their faces with paper fans.

This is a story about a woman named Stephanie Michele, a keeper of the animals at the reserve around the lake. She is a person well acquainted with the secret ways of animals and hurting souls needing a place to just . . . be.

And this is a story about him.

It started that summer two years ago, the one that steamed into Oakland like a thief in the night. It was hot. Children were out of school.

For many days, Stephanie Michele had noticed him sitting there. He didn't smile or talk or play. He just sat for hours alone, and watched the geese. At times he seemed to be listening to them.

"Ain't that peculiar," homeless Mae Marie said as she pushed her shopping cart by him.

Still, he began to feel like a regular there at the lake, like Mae Marie, whose whole life was stuffed right into that old cart, and Willie Jack, who'd been crippled by the war.

"Child, what's your name?" Stephanie Michele asked him one day.

"Fondo," he answered.

"I like that name. Who gave you that name?"

"Don't know."

"Your daddy?"

"Don't got one."

"How about your momma?"

He didn't answer. Just looked away.

"Well, child, I'm glad you're here. Looking at your face starts my day out just fine."

Both of them sat for a while and watched the geese together.

"Looks like you see the same magic in them I do," she remarked.

He smiled for the very first time.

"I'll be feeding them soon. Would you like to come along?" she asked, fully expecting him not to. But he got up and took her hand.

At first, he just stood by her and watched, but then he pitched in and helped her clean the ponds and put out feed and grasses for the other birds.

Then, over by the bridge, the boy stopped. One of the geese seemed dizzy and unsteady on her feet.

"She's blind," Stephanie Michele told him.

Fondo came close to the little goose.

"She does all right, except I have to help her find the pond so she'll get at fresh water and food. Sometimes I hand-feed her," she said as she pushed oatmeal at the goose's beak. "She'll fly someday, though, probably higher and better than the others."

"She just needs a little help now, don't she?" Fondo asked.

Willy Jack passed them just then. "That goose ain't good for nothing," he yelled. "She can't even feed herself . . . how can she fly!"

Fondo held the little goose and rocked her in his arms.

As the weeks passed, Fondo turned up every single day to help Stephanie Michele. They walked together, ate together, and dreamed together. And so it was too that the little blind goose had found a friend. She always seemed to be at Fondo's side.

"She hasn't looked that happy in a very long time," Stephanie Michele remarked.

"She makes me happy, too," Fondo said. "She makes me smile inside." He gestured to where his heart was beating.

Fondo had become such a familiar face there at the lake that even Mae Marie had taken up a great fondness for him. She fussed over his hair whenever she could. And Willy Jack, who yelled at just about everybody, didn't yell so much at Fondo.

Then one day, as the boy was getting ready to leave the park, Stephanie Michele asked him, "Need a lift home?"

Fondo looked troubled for a split second. "I'll be okay," he said, and quickly shuffled off through the gate.

Stephanie Michele watched until she couldn't see him anymore. Then she took a long last look at the sun as it sank into the horizon.

"You listening to that sun again, ain't ya?" Mae Marie asked as she rolled by Stephanie Michele.

"Indeed I am," Stephanie Michele said.

"What do you hear it say?" Willy Jack asked as he joined them.

"It talks to me about the hearts of people folk, and animals, too . . . especially the ones needing one thing or another."

"No way, man. No one can hear the sun," Willy Jack said, gesturing wildly as he walked away.

"I believe you can, Stephanie Michele," Mae Marie finally said. Then she shuffled off behind her cart to find her usual bench to sleep.

Stephanie Michele just sat for a while and listened. Then she put food, which she knew Willy Jack and Mae Marie would be needing later that night, on the porch of the science center, and went home.

The next day, Fondo was waiting at the gate, as he did every morning, to begin his chores with Stephanie Michele. They worked hard together, not saying much but feeling real comfortable with each other. When they finally sat eating their sandwiches, they were surrounded by the geese.

"Did you know all of the geese have names?" Stephanie Michele asked as she threw a piece of bread to a big goose.

"I know the names," he said, and gave a quiet smile.

"How, child? I've never told them to you, have I?"

"They told me."

Willy Jack had taken his usual place on the bench. "Unh-uh. They can't talk, and you can't hear them."

Stephanie Michele put her arm around Fondo. "I don't suppose you can hear that old sun up there, too, can you?" she asked.

"I can," he said as his eyes widened.

"Well, ain't we a pair," Stephanie Michele said.

As the park was closing, Stephanie Michele asked again if she could take Fondo home. Again, he refused.

Before long, Fondo knew the routine of the park better than all of the other workers. Stephanie Michele even gave him an official Parks and Recreation shirt with his name on it. "Because you work so hard," she told him.

Whatever he did, he was never without the little blind goose. She went everywhere with him. When he was measuring mash to feed the birds. When he was filling the pond for the ducks. She seemed always to know where he was, even though she couldn't see him.

"Pretty soon, you're gonna turn into a goose!" Mae Marie said to him one day when all the geese were following him.

"Wish I could," Fondo answered softly.

"Ain't no way, man," Willy Jack yelled and scowled.

The three of them looked up to see a flock of geese take flight with one sweep of their wings, only to circle and settle back onto the surface of the lake.

"We all could fly once," Fondo said as he gazed at the clouds. "We just forgot how. If we'd think hard enough, we'd remember."

"Tell you what, kid," Willy Jack said, "you fly, and I'll start believing in something again."

"Me, too," Mae Marie said as she touched Fondo's cheek, then scurried off with her cart.

"All's you gotta do is believe!" Fondo called after them.

Stephanie Michele put her arm around him.

"Heard them talking about leaving soon," Fondo said as he gestured toward the geese.

"Maybe they'll invite you!" she said, trying to laugh. But then she looked deep into Fondo's eyes and saw that he knew more about flying than anyone she had ever known.

That night when Fondo disappeared through the gate after the park closed, Stephanie Michele followed him. She watched him walk slowly down Grand Avenue, then turn into the settlement-house building. A place for homeless and unwanted children.

Not many mornings after, Fondo met Stephanie Michele at the entrance gate of the park. He seemed worried and distant. He wasn't his usual self.

"They are sending me away," Fondo blurted out. He'd guessed Stephanie Michele knew about the home.

"Away where?" Stephanie Michele asked.

"A permanent place for kids like me. I'm not much on learning. They call me slow."

"Oh, honey, if only all of us could be slow like you," Stephanie Michele said as she hugged him close.

"I failed all the tests they've been giving me. They say I'm a special-needs case."

"Oh, child, you're special all right. The most loving and gentle soul that I have ever known."

"I love it here. Why can't they let me stay here at the park with you and them?" He pointed at the geese.

The next morning when Stephanie Michele got to the lake, it was dark and cloudy. She found Fondo standing at the edge of the pond, arms outstretched, eyes looking at the sky above him.

"He's been like this for hours," Mae Marie said.

"It's real spooky, man. I saw people like this in 'Nam. He's just been standing there," Willy Jack said.

"How long you been here, child?" Stephanie Michele asked as she wrapped her coat around him.

At first he didn't answer. He just kept looking at the sky. Then he said, "I'm leaving."

"I know. I tried to talk to a Doctor Patterson last night when I took you back, but it didn't do any good," Stephanie Michele said.

"No, I'm leaving with them." He gestured to the geese. "They invited me today."

Stephanie Michele pulled him into her arms. "Of course they did, of course they did," she cooed as she rocked him.

The settlement-house people came right to the park and got Fondo. They knew where he'd be.

As the day drew to an end, Stephanie Michele found herself on the bench with Willy Jack and Mae Marie. Just sitting and crying and hoping things could be different.

Willy Jack cried, too. Probably for the first time in many years. Mae Marie talked about her sister in Tulsa. She had never talked about her sister in Tulsa before.

Just then there was a noise in the bushes behind them.

It was Fondo.

"I ran away," he announced.

"Does Doctor Patterson know you're gone?" Stephanie Michele asked.

"Probably by now, but it won't matter. I'm flying away . . . tonight."

"Oh, Fondo," Stephanie Michele said. "I've let you down. I'm so sorry."

"But all of the geese are gone, they already left!" Mae Marie called out.

The lake was strangely empty of geese. There wasn't a one.

Then they heard a sound in the darkness. At first, it was a soft distant symphony of rushing wind, but it built like summer thunder, low, deep, and grand.

Stephanie Michele, Mae Marie, and Willy Jack all squinted to see. The setting sun shone an orange brilliance on the edges of hundreds, thousands, millions of beating wings.

It was the geese, more geese than had ever come to the lake. But they were strangely quiet. There was no honking, no calling between them.

They circled the lake twice, then three times. Finally, as if by command, they glided onto the surface of the lake and shoveled their feet to land on the dark, still water.

Their leader swam to the shore. It was the little blind goose. She bowed her head to Fondo, then stretched out her neck just as he was reaching out his hand to her.

Fondo turned and looked at Stephanie Michele. "It's time to go," he said.

"I know, child," Stephanie Michele said. Her eyes brimmed with tears.

"Keep listening to the sun," he said.

Then he smiled at all of them, and as light as a feather blown by an evening breeze, he simply lifted off from the ground. He hovered there for a fleeting moment, weightless and free, then he gave a nod to the geese. With a call from their leader, there was a wild flurry of wings, waves of rushing water, exuberant honks, and they disappeared into the orange sky.

Then there was only the sound of Mae Marie sighing and Willy Jack laughing. The three of them vowed they would never tell what really happened to Fondo. After all, who would believe such a thing? The settlement-house people, good people, looked for him for a while, then put his name on a long list in a thick dusty file somewhere.

But I know this is a true story because, you see, I know Stephanie Michele. I see her almost every time I walk around Lake Merritt. She still works right there at the science center and bird sanctuary.

You'll know her when you see her; she'll always be with the geese. She's the one looking at the sky. And listening.

For Stephanie Michele Benavidez,
the little blind goose,
and Fondo.

PUFFIN BOOKS
Published by the Penguin Group
Penguin Putnam Books for Young Readers,
345 Hudson Street, New York, New York 10014, U.S.A.
Penguin Books Ltd, 27 Wrights Lane, London W8 5TZ, England
Penguin Books Australia Ltd, Ringwood, Victoria, Australia
Penguin Books Canada Ltd, 10 Alcorn Avenue, Toronto,
Ontario, Canada M4V 3B2
Penguin Books (N.Z.) Ltd, 182-190 Wairau Road,
Auckland 10, New Zealand

Penguin Books Ltd, Registered Offices: Harmondsworth,
Middlesex, England

First published in the United States of America by Philomel Books,
a division of The Putnam & Grosset Group, 1996
Published by Puffin Books, a member of Penguin Putnam Books
for Young Readers, 1999

13 14 15 16 17 18 19 20

THE LIBRARY OF CONGRESS HAS CATALOGED THE PHILOMEL EDITION AS FOLLOWS:
Polacco, Patricia. I can hear the sun: a modern myth / Patricia Polacco. p. cm.
Summary: Stephanie Michele, who cares for animals and listens
to the sun, believes the homeless child, Fondo, when he tells her
that the geese have invited him to fly away with them.
[1. Homeless persons—Fiction. 2. Sun—Fiction. 3. Geese—Fiction.
4. Listening—Fiction.] I. Title. PZ7.P75186Iaaf 1996 [E]—dc20
95-32091 CIP AC ISBN 0-399-22520-X

Puffin Books ISBN 978-0-698-11857-7

Manufactured in China